MW00908083

The Chatterbox Turtle

Story by Cynthia Rider
Pictures by Andrea Petrlik

dingles&company

Turtle lived in a muddy pool.
Lots of animals came to the
pool to drink. Turtle loved to
talk to the animals.

2

"Turtle is a big chatterbox," they said.

3

One day, Turtle saw two geese
by the pool.
"What are you doing here?" he
asked.

4

"We are on our way home," said the geese. "We live far, far away on a beautiful blue lake."

5

Turtle looked at his
muddy pool.
"I wish I could go there,"
he said.

"Why don't you fly back with us?" asked the two geese.
"I can't fly," Turtle told them.

"We'll carry you to the lake," said the geese. "But you must not talk until we get home."

"I won't say one word!" said Turtle.

The geese found a long stick.
They held it in their beaks.

"Hold onto this with your mouth," they said. "And remember! You must not talk. Not a word, or you will fall."

Turtle put the stick in his
mouth, and the two geese flew
up, up into the sky.

As they flew over the trees, two parrots saw them.

14

Turtle wanted to shout back to them.
Just in time, he remembered not to talk.

The monkeys saw Turtle, too. They waved their paws at him.
"You look silly," they shouted.

Turtle wanted to shout. Just in time, he remembered not to talk.

"Look! Turtle has to keep his mouth closed." Snake laughed. "I bet you can't keep your mouth closed, Turtle. You can't stop talking."

18

"Yes I can!"
shouted Turtle.

Down,

down,

down

he fell.

Bump!

Bump!

Bump!

he went.

21

The animals rushed to see if he was all right. Turtle grinned up at them. "You were right," he said. "I can't stop talking."

"But now that I've been flying," he said, "I've got even more to talk about!"

And he went all the way home
to his muddy pool.

24